The Licia & Mason Beekley Community Library

10 central avenue . p.o. box 247
new hartford . connecticut 06057
860 379-7235

D1365791

DATE DUE

www.ziplinebook.com

For Ella

If you peek at my middle
in the center of my chest,

you'll notice something different,
it's not like all the rest.

Some will wonder silently,
while others may just stare,

but what you must want to know,
"How did that line get there?"

and I didn't get a scratch
showing a lion who is cool.

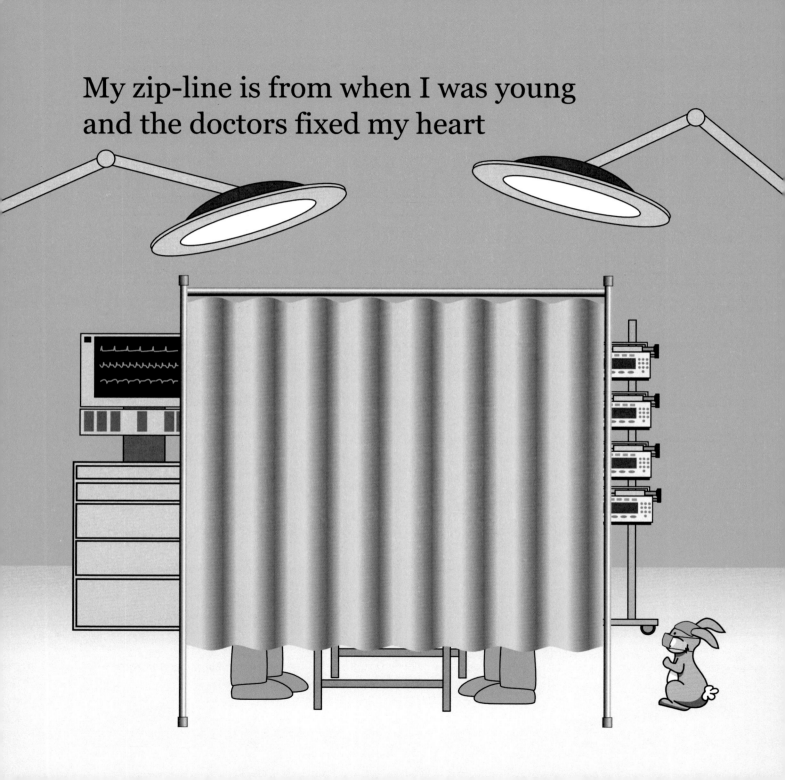

the scar that was left there
is my personal work of art.

"Zip-line"

The zip-line is my trophy
for being strong and brave

my surgery lasted hours
and my recovery took days.

There were pumps, tubes and wires
and I needed lots of rest,

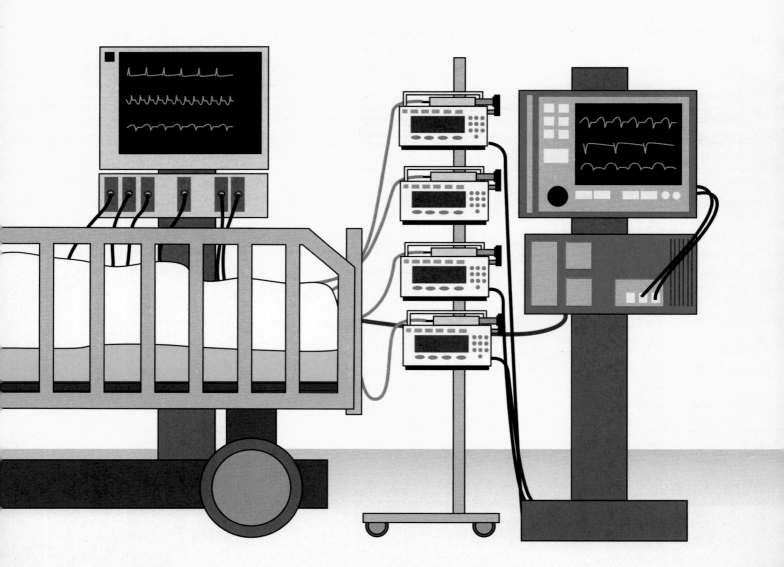

everyone worked really hard
to help me be my best.

Now I'm strong and healthy
I'm really doing fine

When I play in the sprinkler
or wear my suit at the pool

you might notice my zip-line
and think it is pretty cool.

So ask me and I'll tell you
my story and my name,

and though we might look different there
we're otherwise the same.

Now let's go have fun and play
or challenge me to a race,

there's nothing that can stop me
my heart's keeping perfect pace.

www.ziplinebook.com

Made in the USA
Middletown, DE
29 March 2019